BEN 10 RETURNS: PART 1 & PART 2

EGMONT

We bring stories to life

First published in Great Britain 2009
by Egmont UK Limited
239 Kensington High Street
London W8 6SA

ISBN 978 1 4052 4799 3
1 3 5 7 9 10 8 6 4 2

Printed in Italy

BEN 10 RETURNS: PART 1

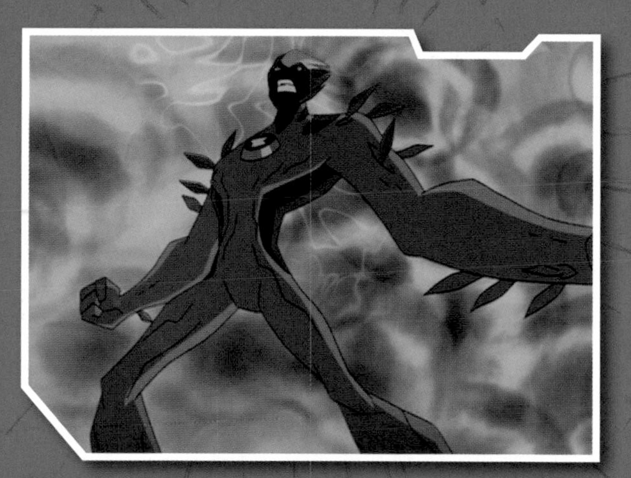

Ben Tennyson is now 15 years old, and it's time for him to go hero again! Armed with a new Omnitrix, there are some brand new awesome alien dudes for Ben to get to grips with, and some deadly villains for him to defeat. Gwen is determined to help Ben out, and her own magical powers will prove invaluable . . .

Inside the HighBreed base, a DNAlien approaches the HighBreed Leader.

You may speak to me, half-breed vermin.

Someone has been leaking the details of our secret operations to the authorities. We have found the source of the leak.

His name is Max Tennyson. We've had trouble with him before.

Then let this be the final time he troubles us. Destroy him!

Meanwhile, 15 year-old Ben Tennyson is on his way home after playing in a football match. He cycles over to see his Grandpa Max at the trailer park.

Grandpa Max? Open up, it's me.

Ben let's himself in. Inside, the Rustbucket's a mess and there's no sign of Grandpa Max.

Suddenly, a strange-looking creature appears behind Ben. Ben swings round and comes face-to-face with a DNAlien. Its body splits open and a bunch of tentacles falls out and darts towards Ben at speed!

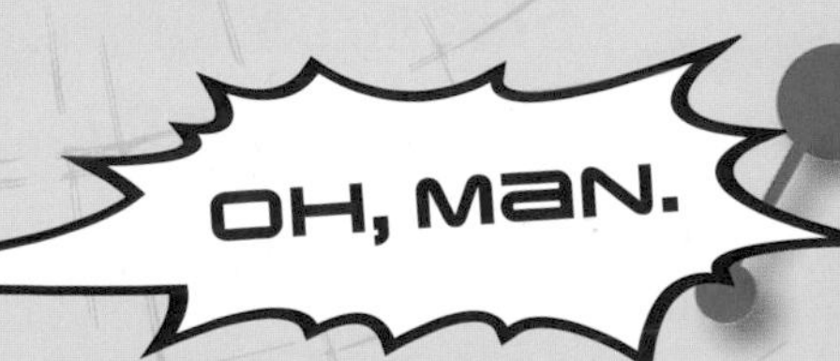

Ben dodges the tentacles as they shoot out, and ducks as the DNAlien throws a punch. Suddenly, Ben spots a fire extinguisher. He grabs it, and fires it at the DNAlien, covering it in foam.

Peek-a-boo!

The DNAlien escapes through the front window, smashing the glass.

Left on his own again, Ben flips a switch on the dashboard, and a tube shoots out. It's a Communicator. Ben activates the device. An image of Grandpa Max appears!

Hello, Ben. I left this recording for you. I'm in a bit of a situation, but it's nothing I can't handle. There's renewed alien activity on Earth. I'm investigating.
And don't worry about the Omnitrix. I have it, and it's completely safe.

Ben grabs the Communicator and rushes home. He runs straight into his bedroom and rifles through a drawer. He's looking for his alien-transforming watch – the Omnitrix.

Grandpa Max says he's got the Omnitrix, but I know it's in here somewhere.

Sure enough, Ben finds the Omnitrix, safely hidden under a deck of cards in one of his drawers.

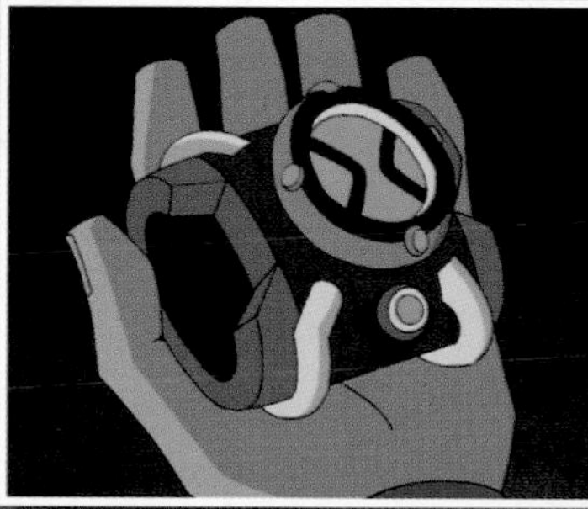

What are you trying to tell me, Grandpa?

Ben goes to find his cousin, Gwen. She's in the school gym, and has just finished competing in a karate competition – she won, of course!

Grandpa doesn't have the Omnitrix. You do.

Yeah, he's sending me some kind of message. I think he wants me to put it on again.

You earned the chance to have a normal life. Put the Omnitrix back on, and that's pretty much it for normal.

But if Grandpa needs my help . . .

Suddenly the door swings open, and a dark figure appears.

The Omnitrix ain't yours. Give it to me now.

Or what?

Or . . . this. Don't make me use it on you.

The dark figure pulls off a mask, revealing that he is an alien! And he's aiming a gun at Ben and Gwen . . .

Gwen decides it's time to use her magical superpowers! She creates two round balls of sizzling energy, and fires an energy beam at the guy.

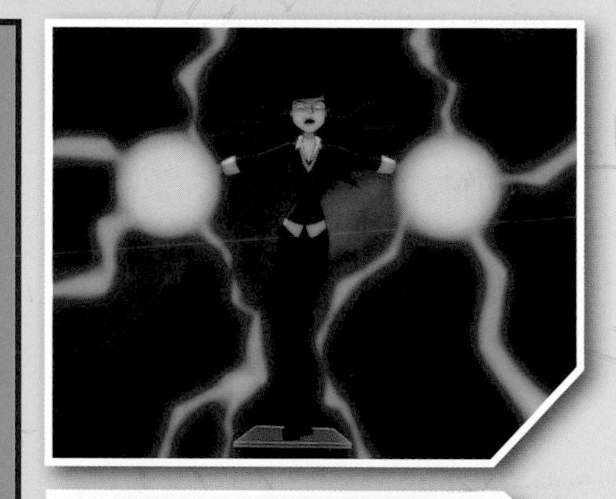

Gwen has trapped the alien in a powerful energy orb! He angrily tells them that he's called the Magister.

I'm a deputy agent of the Plumbers, an intergalactic law enforcement organisation.

I know who they are. My Grandpa Max used to be a Plumber.

Wait. He's your grandfather? You're the legendary Ben Tennyson? I thought you were just some kid who'd snatched the Omnitrix. I owe you an apology. Get me out of this thing, then maybe we can find your grandpa together.

Thinking it's time he put the Omnitrix on again, Ben clasps it to his wrist.

Later, Ben, Gwen and the Magister are down by the docks. The Magister's explained that they're lying in wait for the Forever Knights, a group of criminals who trade in alien technology.

They're supposed to show up here tonight to receive a shipment of illegal alien tech. Wait – someone's coming!

Two trucks roar to a halt. Then, a green car pulls up, and a young guy hops out. He is brokering a weapons deal.

As promised, four dozen brand new laser lances. With an ether point energy module and an antenna focus emitter.

It's Kevin E. Levin! He's got superpowers. I fought him when we were kids. He got trapped in the Null Void – kind of an extra-dimensional jail.

Kevin takes a laser lance out from its case and fires it at a wall.

It's good for thirty-five minutes of continuous fire at point-six terawatts.

The wall explodes in a ball of flames.

Is that good? You tell me.

The Magister is furious. He tells Ben and Gwen that the lances are level five technology, and planet Earth only has level two! He sneaks up on the men.

Hands above your heads, air breathers. By authority of the Plumbers, you're all busted.

Suddenly, the men selling the laser guns and standing next to Kevin, rip off masks and reveal themselves to be DNAliens!

Ummm, and there are some other guys behind us. We are toast.

The crew buying the weapons, the Forever Knights, are right behind Ben, Gwen and the Magister!

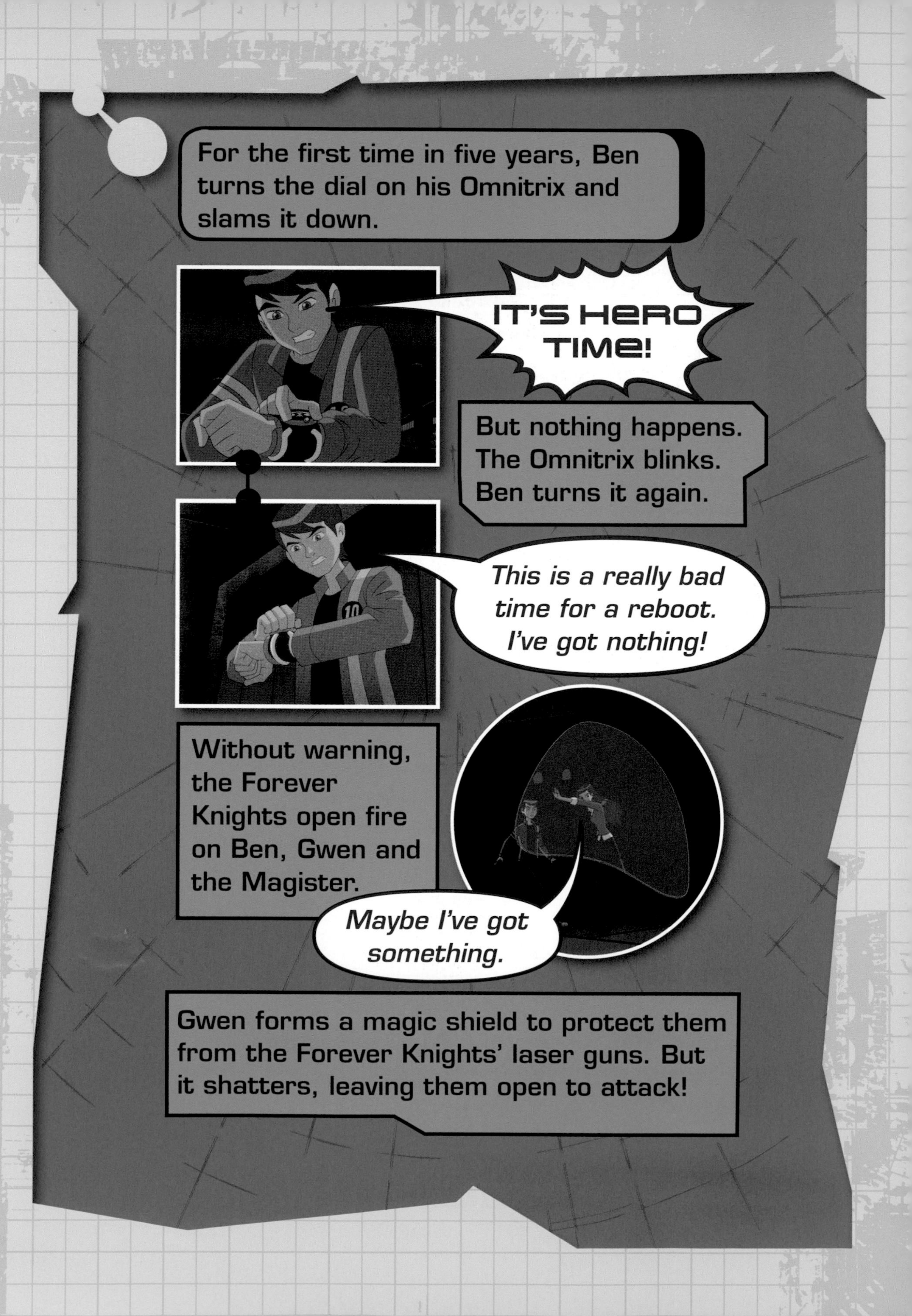
For the first time in five years, Ben turns the dial on his Omnitrix and slams it down.
IT'S HERO TIME!
But nothing happens. The Omnitrix blinks. Ben turns it again.
This is a really bad time for a reboot. I've got nothing!
Without warning, the Forever Knights open fire on Ben, Gwen and the Magister.
Maybe I've got something.
Gwen forms a magic shield to protect them from the Forever Knights' laser guns. But it shatters, leaving them open to attack!

The DNAliens start spitting sticky green goo at Gwen and the Magister. Gross! They're trapped and cannot move.

Ben's still desperately trying to work the Omnitrix. Suddenly, it glows green and shrinks on to his wrist. Ben scrolls through the alien options . . .

I don't recognise any of these guys. But this one looks pretty good.

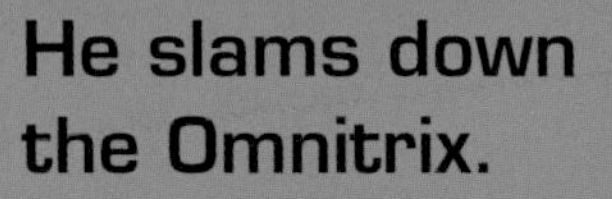

He slams down the Omnitrix.

And a surge of powerful energy flows through Ben's body.

Ben transforms into Swampfire!

GET AWAY FROM MY FRIENDS!
Cut it out, that tickles!

Swampfire punches the DNAliens, knocking them down. Terrified, they speed off in their trucks. The Forever Knights fire laser blasts at Swampfire.

Suddenly, a laser severs Swampfire's arm, but vines shoot out from the arm and it re-attaches itself back on to Swampfire!

You guys are in so much trouble!

There's a face-off between Kevin and Swampfire. Using his own superpowers, Kevin touches a metal cable on the ground, and he slowly turns to metal.

You trapped me in the Null Void. And you ruined my deal today. I want revenge.

Kevin picks up a giant crate, and hurls it towards Swampfire.

This is what happens when you mess with me.

Swampfire blasts the crate back at Kevin! Kevin turns back to his normal form and is knocked out cold.

Meanwhile, the Forever Knights have escaped with their new weapons, and the DNAliens have run off with the money.

Swampfire turns back into Ben. Kevin comes round, but the Magister has trapped him.

The technology of those weapons is way too advanced for humans. They shouldn't even be on this planet.

So? How's that my problem?

While we were fighting, the Forever Knights got away with a crate full of 'em.

Kevin, people could get hurt.

You set up the deal. You're going to tell us where they are.

You don't have to convince me. Those guys ran off before I got paid. I'm happy to help find those deadbeats.

Now that Kevin has been recruited, he, Ben, Gwen and the Magister hop into Kevin's car and speed off into the night. They're on the hunt for the Forever Knights . . .

In the car, the Magister talks about what's been happening.

There's been a lot of alien activity on Earth lately. Don't know why. Your grandfather thought maybe the weapons deal would lead us to something. Now he's missing.

I just wish Grandpa was here. He would know what to do. He always knows what to do.

Well he ain't. You're the one with the Omnitrix. You're going to have to figure out how to get things done on your own.

This is it. We've arrived.

The gang arrive at the Forever Knights' base. It's a castle! Using her magic, Gwen pulls the drawbridge down, and they walk inside.

Ben backs into a suit of armour that crumbles to the ground, making a loud clattering sound.

CRASH!

C'mon man. What are you doing?

Sorry. Guess I'm just a little . . . paranoid.

From behind Ben, a giant dragon has emerged out of the gloom!

ROARRRR!

TO BE CONTINUED . . .

SWAMPFIRE

Swampfire is like an extremely strong walking compost heap! How many times does he appear in this wordsearch? His name can run up, down, forwards, backwards and diagonally.

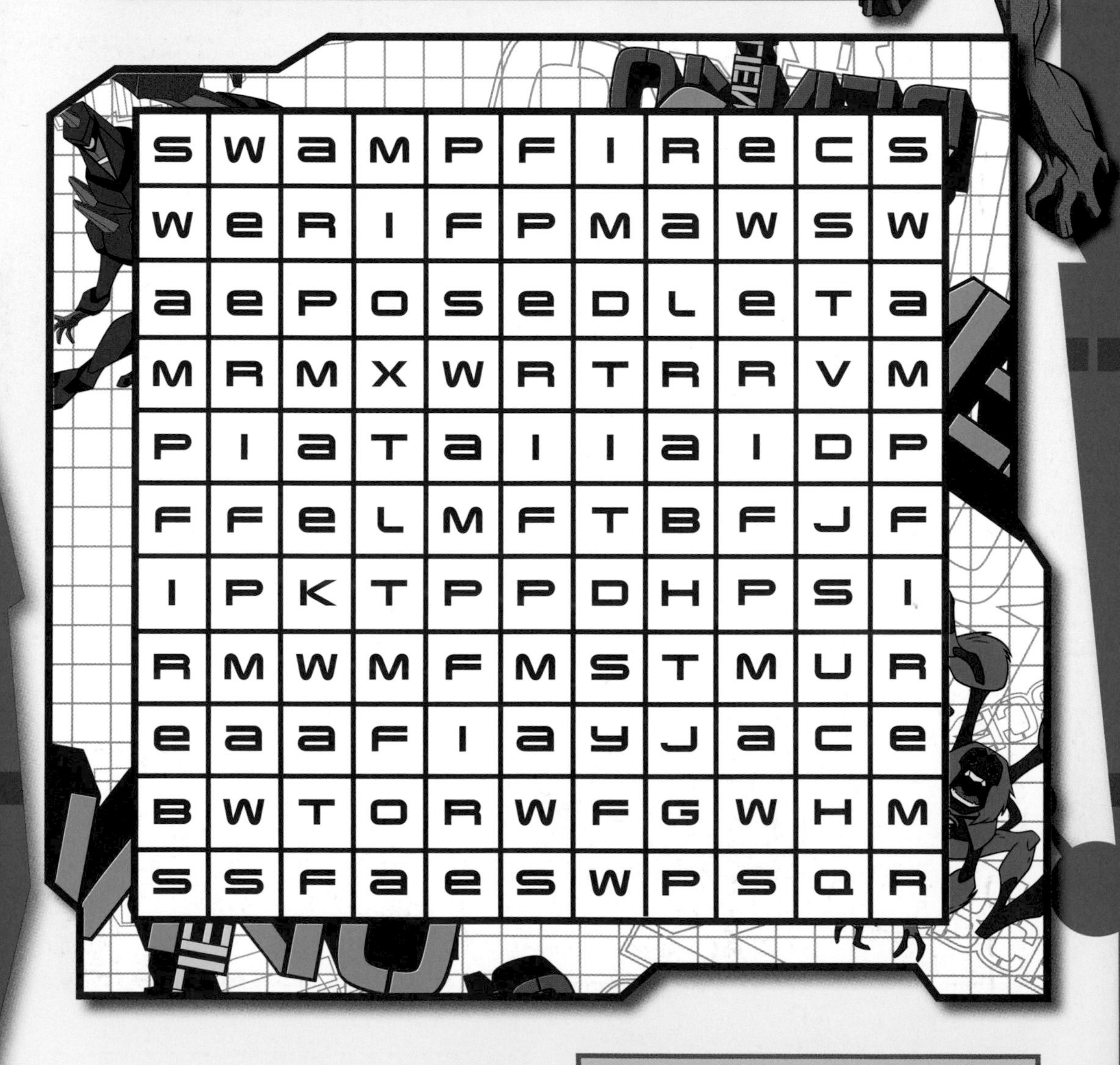

S	W	a	M	P	F	I	R	e	C	S
W	e	R	I	F	P	M	a	W	S	W
a	e	P	O	S	e	D	L	e	T	a
M	R	M	X	W	R	T	R	R	V	M
P	I	a	T	a	I	I	a	I	D	P
F	F	e	L	M	F	T	B	F	J	F
I	P	K	T	P	P	D	H	P	S	I
R	M	W	M	F	M	S	T	M	U	R
e	a	a	F	I	a	Y	J	a	C	e
B	W	T	O	R	W	F	G	W	H	M
S	S	F	a	e	S	W	P	S	Q	R

Answer: Swampfire appears 9 times.

ECHO ECHO
ROUND-UP
Count how many times Echo Echo appears here. Write your answer in the box!
ECHO ECHO APPEARS
TIMES.
Answer: Echo Echo appears 26 times.

ALIEN MATCH

Can you tell which of Ben's aliens is which, from their shadows? Use lines to join each alien shadow to its correct colour image. Bonus points if you know each alien's name!

Answers: A–3 (Big Chill), B–4 (Brainstorm), C–2 (Chromastone), D–5 (Humungousaur), E–1 (Jetray).

© CN
© CN
© CN
© CN
© CN
© CN
© CN
© CN
© CN
© CN
© CN
© CN
© CN
© CN
© CN
© CN

© CN
© CN
© CN
© CN
© CN
© CN
© CN
© CN
© CN
© CN
© CN
© CN
© CN
© CN
© CN
© CN

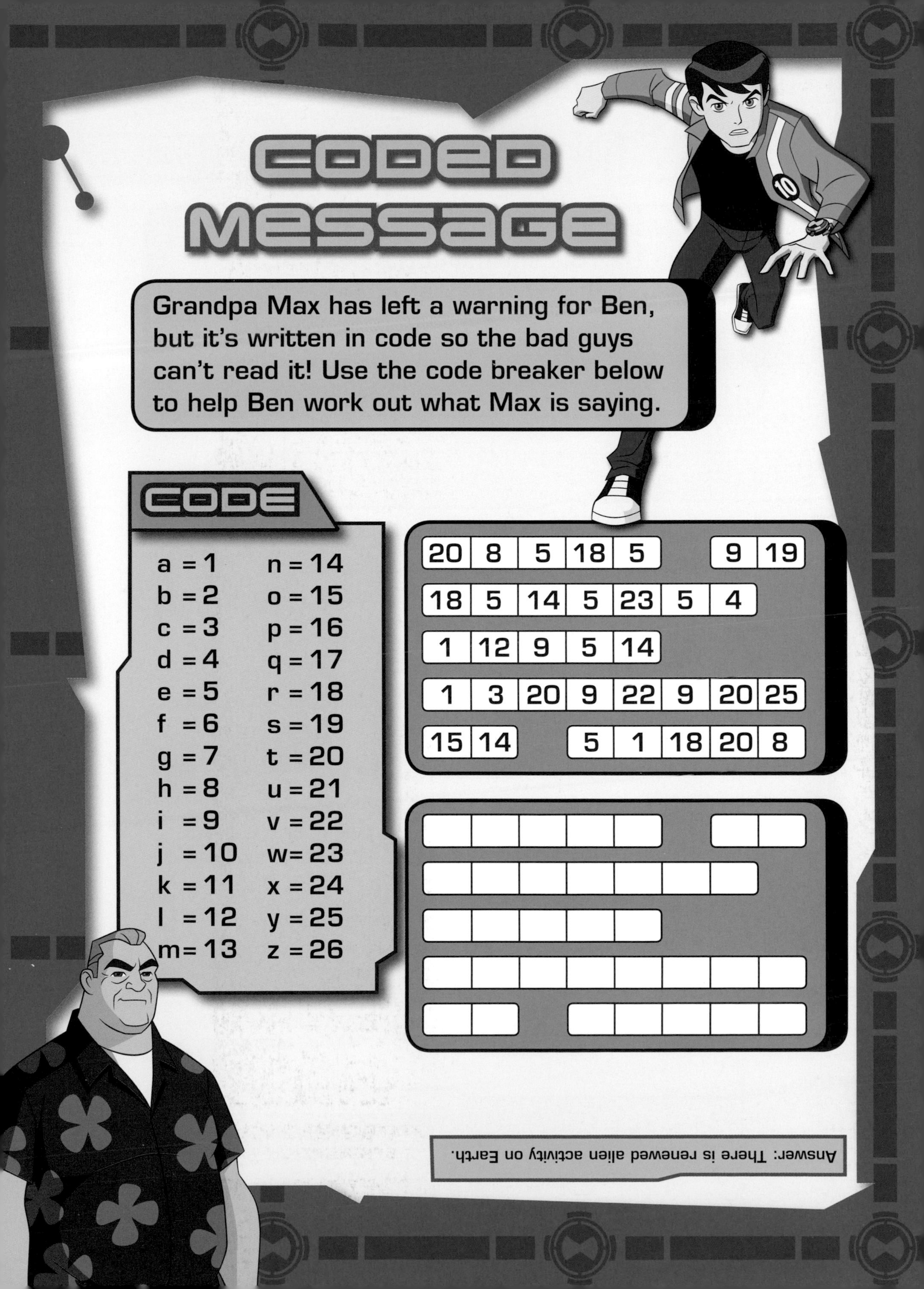
CODED MESSAGE
Grandpa Max has left a warning for Ben, but it's written in code so the bad guys can't read it! Use the code breaker below to help Ben work out what Max is saying.
CODE
a = 1
b = 2
c = 3
d = 4
e = 5
f = 6
g = 7
h = 8
i = 9
j = 10
k = 11
l = 12
m = 13
n = 14
o = 15
p = 16
q = 17
r = 18
s = 19
t = 20
u = 21
v = 22
w = 23
x = 24
y = 25
z = 26
20 8 5 18 5 9 19
18 5 14 5 23 5 4
1 12 9 5 14
1 3 20 9 22 9 20 25
15 14 5 1 18 20 8
Answer: There is renewed alien activity on Earth.

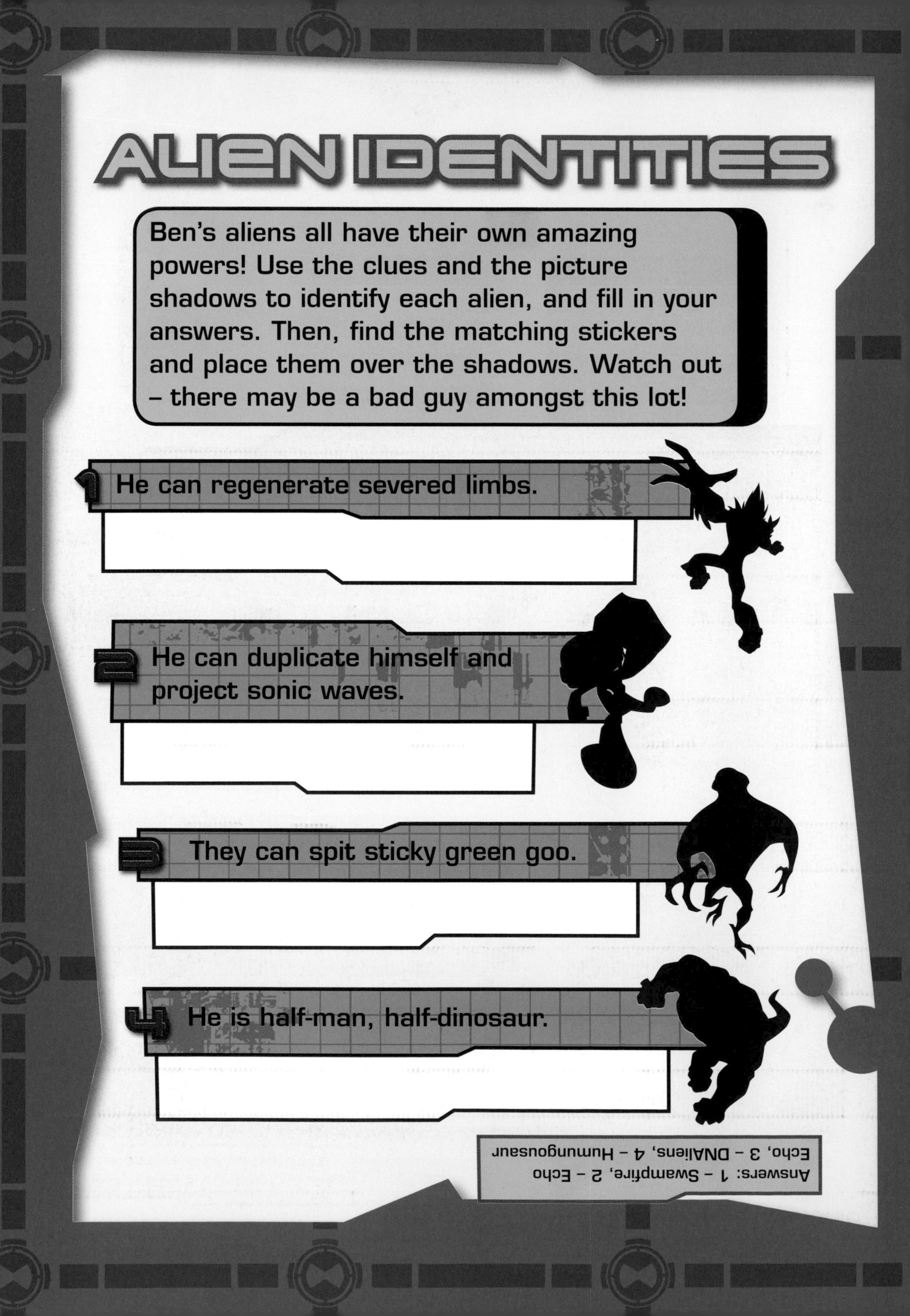

ALIEN IDENTITIES

Ben's aliens all have their own amazing powers! Use the clues and the picture shadows to identify each alien, and fill in your answers. Then, find the matching stickers and place them over the shadows. Watch out – there may be a bad guy amongst this lot!

1 He can regenerate severed limbs.

2 He can duplicate himself and project sonic waves.

3 They can spit sticky green goo.

4 He is half-man, half-dinosaur.

Answers: 1 – Swampfire, 2 – Echo Echo, 3 – DNAliens, 4 – Humungousaur

HUMUNGOUSAUR

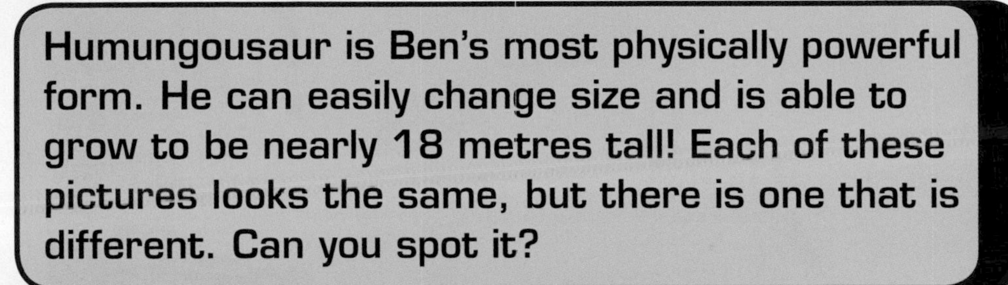

Humungousaur is Ben's most physically powerful form. He can easily change size and is able to grow to be nearly 18 metres tall! Each of these pictures looks the same, but there is one that is different. Can you spot it?

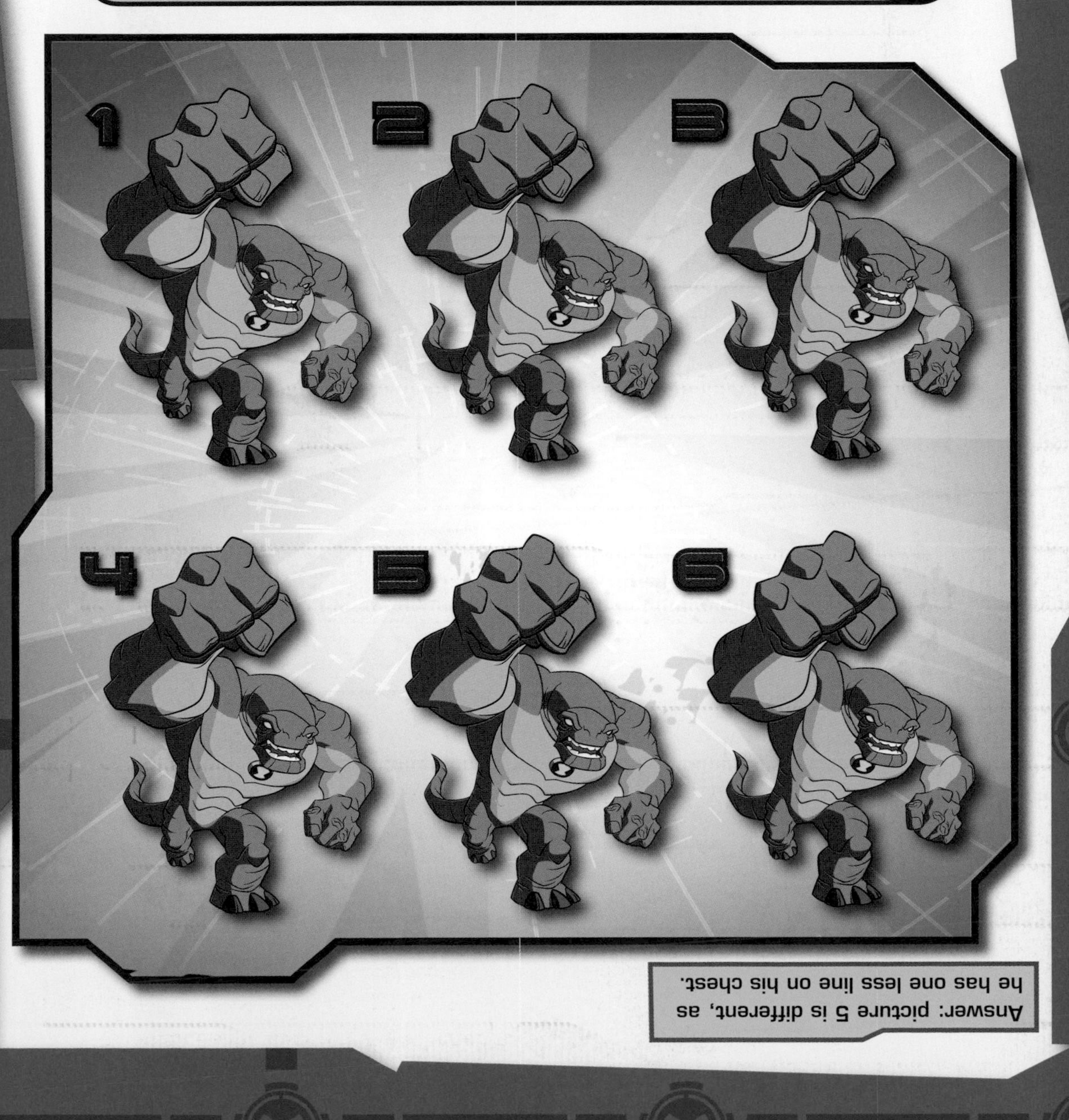

Answer: picture 5 is different, as he has one less line on his chest.

BEN 10 ALIEN FORCE™

On their quest to find Grandpa Max, Ben and Gwen have joined forces with the Magister and Kevin E. Levin. After coming face-to-face with the DNAliens and the Forever Knights for the very first time, the gang have now made it to the Forever Knights' castle, where they're all being eyeballed by one enormous, scary and hungry looking creature . . .

Inside the Forever Knights' castle, Ben, Gwen and the Magister are being chased by a huge, unfriendly dragon.

The Forever Knights also appear, with their guns drawn.

Nobody move. Hands on your head.

Kevin hurls a lump of gravel at the Knights, and they open fire.

Gwen creates a magical shield which deflects the Forever Knights' laser beams back towards them. Meanwhile, the dragon is still charging towards the gang.

It's definitely hero time!

Ben clicks on his Omnitrix and slams it down.

Energy surges through Ben's body and he transforms into Echo Echo, an alien that can duplicate himself as many times as he likes!

Echo Echo Echo Echo Echo Echo Echo Echo.

ECHO ECHO!

The mini Echo Echoes lunge on to the dragon, pulling him down.

Got him. Got him. Got him.

Meanwhile, the Forever Knights are still fighting Kevin and the Magister.

Don't do it!
It's busted.

The Magister fires his gun at a Forever Knight, and the bad guy falls backwards, dropping his laser. The laser fizzes with electricity, but the Knight picks it up and aims it at Kevin.

But the Knight pulls the trigger and he is suddenly engulfed in a large red orb – a huge electric shock. He collapses to the ground.

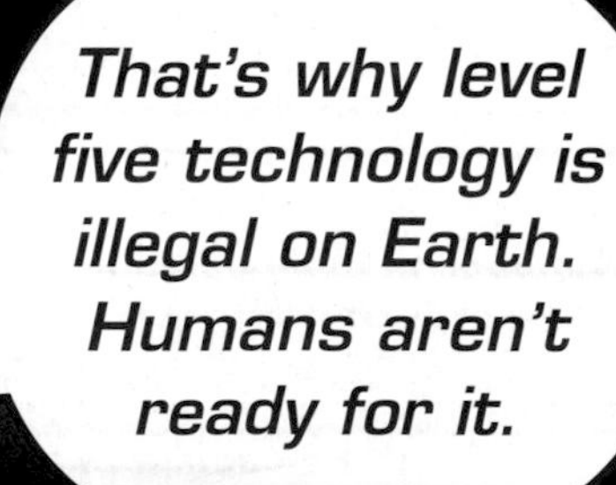

That's why level five technology is illegal on Earth. Humans aren't ready for it.
Thanks, I owe you one.

Gwen uses her magic to pulverise the Knights. A whole bunch of them lie unconscious all around her.

And Echo Echo is still fighting the dragon.

Echo Echo opens his mouth to project some sonic waves. Gwen, Kevin and the Magister cover their ears. Echo Echo throws his high-pitched sound at the dragon which roars and then explodes into pieces.

You could warn us when you're gonna make that noise!

Echo Echo then shatters all the Knights' weapons before transforming back into Ben. He looks at the Magister.

Hey, are you okay? There's water leaking out of your suit.
That's not water. Ben, if you want to help me, finish the job. You have to find where the level five tech is coming from.

Suddenly very weak, the injured Magister collapses.

Your grandpa was on the trail of an alien conspiracy. He was working undercover. If you crack this case, maybe you can find Max and save Earth.
I can't do it without Grandpa. I don't know how.
You are Ben Tennyson. You can do anything.

And then, the Magister evaporates, until there's nothing left.
No!
I'm gonna need help.
You know I'm here for you.
Kevin, there's no money in this, but –
I'm in.

The gang drive off. They haven't gone far when Gwen starts floating above the road in front of the car, with one of the laser guns.

I should be able to trace the vibrations from this laser lance back to the people who used to own it.

I thought I destroyed all those things.

I kept one as a souvenir. Lucky, huh?

Hey, it's working. Follow me.

I'll follow you anywhere.

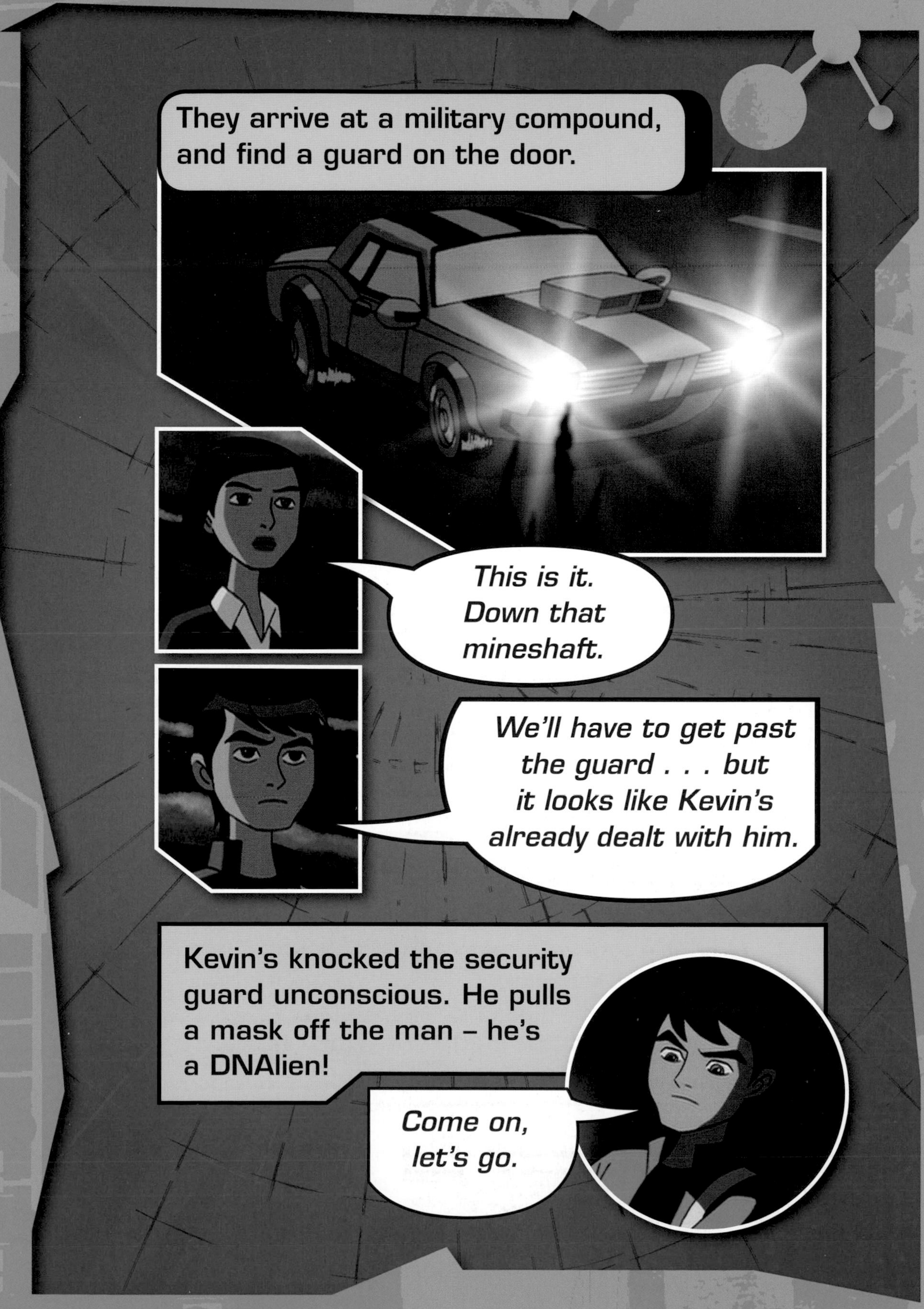

They arrive at a military compound, and find a guard on the door.

This is it. Down that mineshaft.

We'll have to get past the guard . . . but it looks like Kevin's already dealt with him.

Kevin's knocked the security guard unconscious. He pulls a mask off the man – he's a DNAlien!

Come on, let's go.

Ben, Gwen and Kevin head down the mineshaft. The lift takes them to the ground floor. They step outside and gasp. A spaceship is looming up ahead of them!

It's the HighBreed mother ship! Grandpa Max has to be in there. How does this mask work again?

Ben is holding up the mask that Kevin took from the guard.

Photonic displacement. You can set it to make you look like whatever you want.

Ben puts on the mask and changes into a DNAlien.

Some DNAliens are pushing trolleys up a ramp towards the mother ship. Gwen grabs a spare trolley, and she and Kevin hop in and hide. Their very own 'Ben DNAlien' pushes them into the ship.

The trolley stops and Gwen and Kevin hop out. Ben pulls off his mask. Gwen's eyes flash pink as she scans the area for Grandpa Max.

I'm sorry, Ben. Grandpa was here a couple of weeks ago, but he's not here now.

So now what? We just get out of here, right?

Wrong. We're gonna finish this mission.

Suddenly, they hear a DNAlien talking. Looking up, they see more than just one looking down on them . . .

The DNAliens start hurling sticky goo at Ben, Gwen and Kevin. Gwen quickly forms one of her magic shields.

It's hero time!

A surge of energy pushes through Ben's body, and he transforms into the huge half-man, half-dinosaur Humungousaur!

ROARRRRRR!

HUMUNGOUSAUR!

Humungousaur charges at the DNAliens and they flee. Kevin absorbs some metal from the floor.

Hey, save some villains for me!

Humungousaur, Gwen and Kevin fight the DNAliens. The villains are no match for Humungousaur's brutal strength and they are soon all knocked down.

Suddenly, a HighBreed Commander appears out of the gloom . . .

What are you lower life forms doing on my ship?

Did you just call me a lower life form?

I'm pretty sure he did.

You vermin dare to mock a HighBreed Commander?

Kevin charges at the HighBreed, who swats him away easily. Gwen fires some magic cuffs out at the Commander, but he pulls his way out of them and flings Gwen against the wall.

He's too strong. I'll hold him off. You guys, get outside. Kevin, get Gwen out of here.

Kevin snatches Gwen and they run out.

The HighBreed Commander throws a punch at Humungousaur, knocking him away. He then grabs Humungousaur's tail and swings him between the walls. Humungousaur crashes to the ground.

You've ruined everything. By discovering this location, you've set our plans back months.

Now I'll have to move my ship, find a new hiding place. I have to sterilise the area, and destroy all life within five miles of here. No witnesses will live to tell the tale.

You can't!

I can and I will.

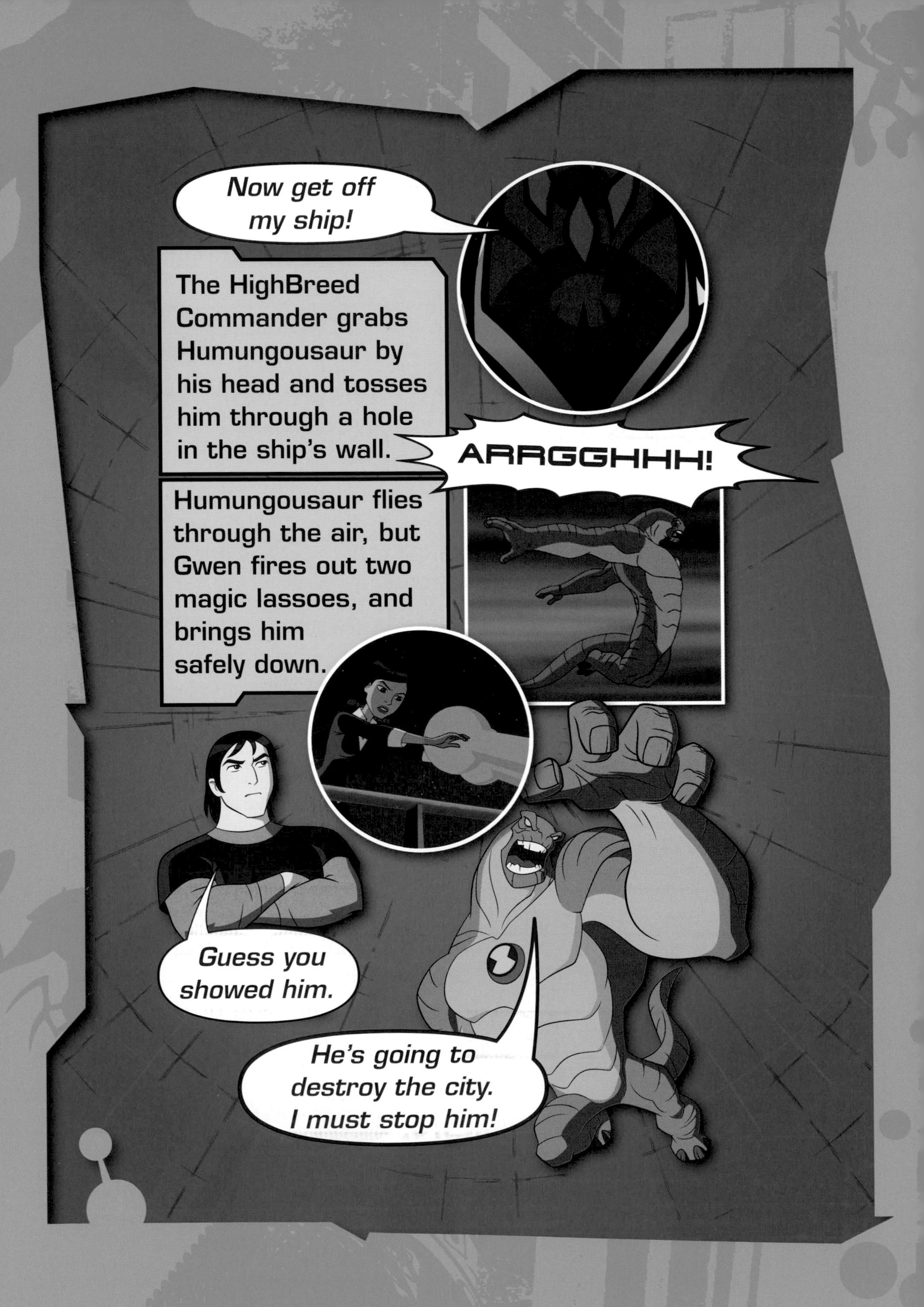
Now get off my ship!
The HighBreed Commander grabs Humungousaur by his head and tosses him through a hole in the ship's wall.
ARRGGHHH!
Humungousaur flies through the air, but Gwen fires out two magic lassoes, and brings him safely down.
Guess you showed him.
He's going to destroy the city. I must stop him!

There's a whirring noise as the ship begins to charge up. It's launching into the air. Humungousaur grows ten times his own size and charges towards it.

You got yourself a BIG problem!

As the ship breaks through the ground, Humungousaur leaps on top of it. He grabs hold of the ship as it soars up into the night sky!

Meanwhile, the DNAliens onboard the ship are preparing to fire the ship's laser beam down on the city below. It will destroy everything in its path.

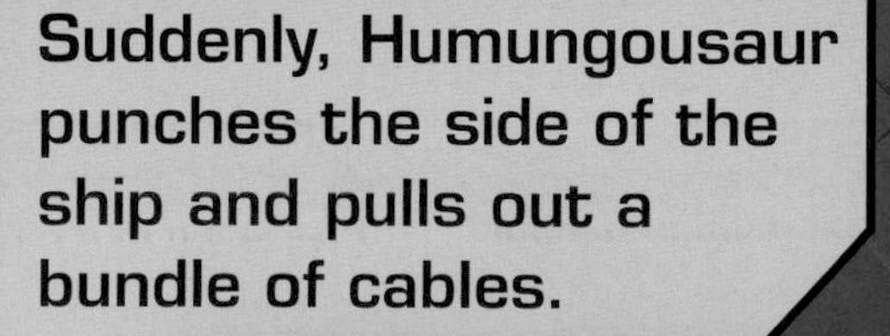

Suddenly, Humungousaur punches the side of the ship and pulls out a bundle of cables.

C'MON. C'MON. C'MON.

The laser approaches a hospital below, but then the beam stops. It flickers and vanishes. Humungousaur plummets to the ground. As he lands, he leaves a huge crater in the earth.

In the distance there's a massive explosion as the mother ship loses control and crashes into the mountains. Gwen and Kevin come running over.

Not fun. Hey, how'd you find me?

We found the big trench you dug over there!

You okay?

Humungousaur skinned his knee. And it's still skinned now I've turned back. Weird.

So, what happens now?

We keep looking for Grandpa Max. Kevin, I want to say thanks. We wouldn't have made it without you.

You still won't make it without me. I'm seeing this through to the end.

And so Ben, Gwen and Kevin shake on it. Meanwhile, inside the HighBreed base . . .

You may speak to me, half-breed vermin.

Max Tennyson continues to evade us. And our supply ship was destroyed in a fight with Ben Tennyson. He has the Omnitrix.

Ben 10 is back. But he has no idea what he's up against, this time. No idea at all.

YOU HAVE READ THE BOOK BUT DO YOU KNOW EVERYTHING ABOUT BEN 10? SIMPLY ANSWER THESE TWO QUESTIONS AT:

TO WIN A BEN 10 GOODY BAG WORTH £20 EVERY MONTH! *
YOU CAN FIND THE ANSWERS IN THE BOOK, SO IF YOU GET STUCK, SIMPLY GO BACK AND CHECK.

QUESTION 1: WHERE IN BEN'S BEDROOM IS THE OMNITRIX HIDDEN?

QUESTION 2: WHICH ALIEN DOES BEN TRANSFORM INTO TO BRING DOWN THE DRAGON AT THE FOREVER KNIGHTS' BASE?

TERMS & CONDITIONS APPLY, SEE ONLINE
*THIS PROMOTION EXPIRES ON 31.12.2009